The story so far...

Mysti and her fairy girl Ella have become friends, and take great care to keep Mysti's magical powers secret from their friends. This can be difficult as Mysti is determined, more and more, to become part of the gang and make the most of her half-human genes.

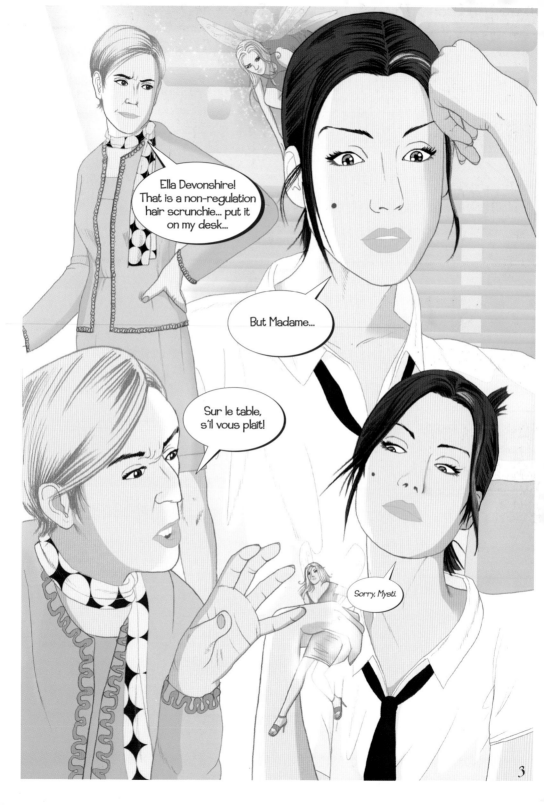

3

5

7

8

12

17

25

I'm glad you've seen sense, Ella.

Well, I thought about it and I'm sure you know best... I should be prepared to make this sacrifce for my GCSEs. After all, they are the most important thing in my life right now.

Sorry Kenzie, Danny, Orlando...

Exactly. I'll get in touch with Miss Ogronski right away.

Ella's room...

What about this one? Mysti? What's wrong?

Paris

33

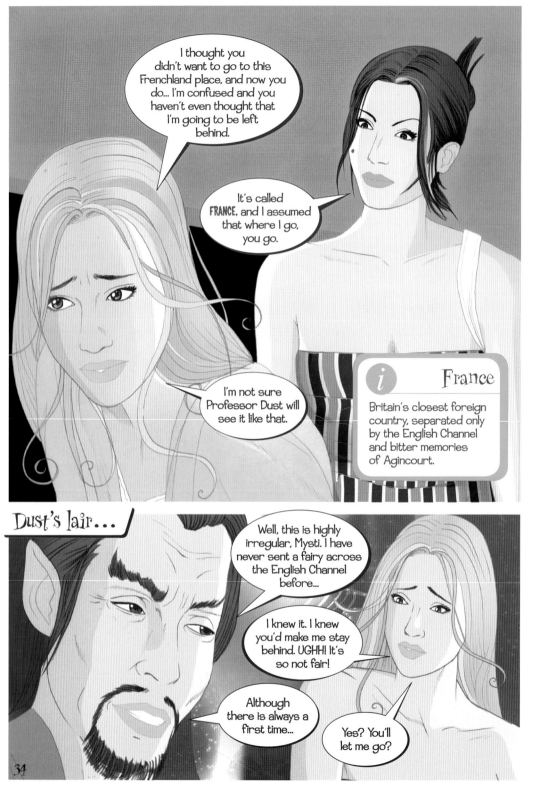

I thought you didn't want to go to this Frenchland place, and now you do... I'm confused and you haven't even thought that I'm going to be left behind.

It's called FRANCE, and I assumed that where I go, you go.

I'm not sure Professor Dust will see it like that.

i France

Britain's closest foreign country, separated only by the English Channel and bitter memories of Agincourt.

Dust's lair...

Well, this is highly irregular, Mysti. I have never sent a fairy across the English Channel before...

I knew it. I knew you'd make me stay behind. UGHH! It's so not fair!

Although there is always a first time...

Yes? You'll let me go?

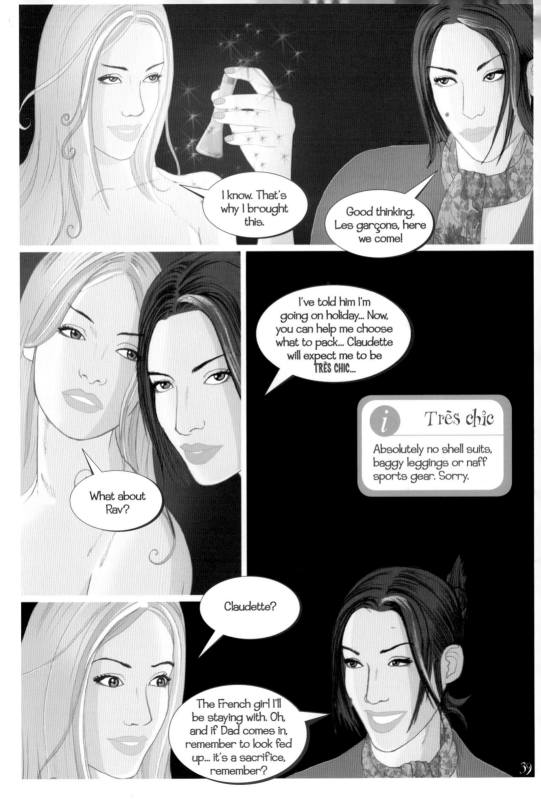

39

Prof. D's study...

Mysti has always been a little...

Impetuous?

...a little like yourself, Tatiana. Say nothing of the fairy we have in mind for her, or she's sure to resist.

We must hope she realises all by herself that Storm is the perfect match for her.

40

Outside school...

41

Cross-channel ferry...

DUTY FREE

Mmm...
I think I am...

Eau So Sexy...

i In loco parentis

Unlike locomotive (which is a train), this is when the teachers officially replace your parents. Pretty scary. No wonder they say it in Latin.

Come on, we're **IN LOCO PARENTIS**... we mustn't let them out of our sight. Oh good, they're going to the disco.

Disco...

I think we've given them the slip.

I'm sure I saw Mysti and Ella come in here... Mmm, what's that smell?

It's coming from over there...

Must be some gorgeous French girl wearing expensive perfume.

45

47

51

53

End of act one

Bonjour, Mysti! Enchantée.

Hi, Celandine... it's great to meet a real French fairy...

Claudette's home, outside Paris...

Welcome, Ella... I hope you'll enjoy your stay. We thought you'd like to start with a typical day on the farm.

57

63

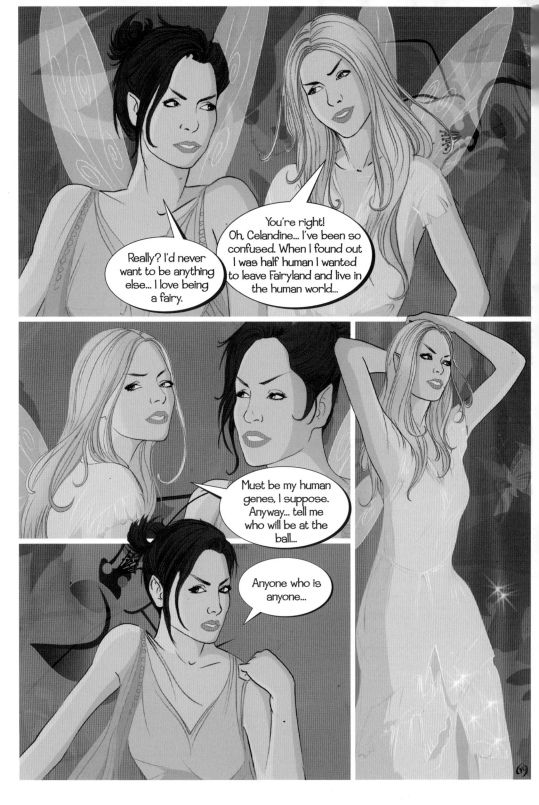

73

I bet you'd all like...

To stare at this all day, yes. We're going to stare at the MONA LISA all day...

i Mona Lisa

A beautiful painting, by Leonardo da Vinci - possibly the most famous in the world. Not to be confused with the Moaner Ella, which we've been seeing throughout the book...

Fairyland, Paris...

83

89

93

95

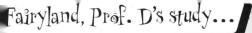

Tatiana, have you heard? Saber has become head of the fairy counsel.

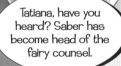

Tatiana, my dear, you must honour me with dinner this evening.

Oh, I remember him, he was quite the charmer.

Meanwhile, in Saber's lair...

We must watch Miss Rainbowfrost carefully. Her closeness to humans is a concern to me, Perry.

Ella's house...

Au revoir, Madame Devonshire. I am sorry to be leaving. I 'ad a great time.

Any time, Claudette. Come see us again.

I have some small gifts for you all.

103

105

107

Mysti and Ella are back in England for
the next instalment in their crazy adventures.

But Mysti's trapped on Earth.
How is she going to cope
with the change to her magic?

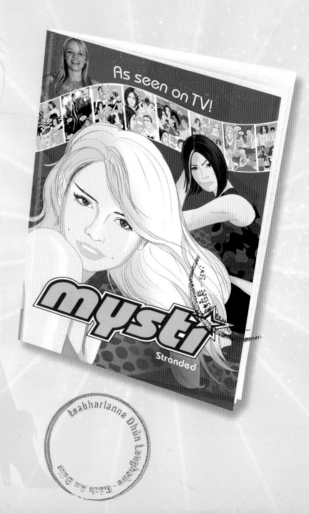

As seen on TV!

mysti

Stranded

All my adventures are now
available to buy from my website
www.mysti.co.uk